A Shark
Out of Water

A Shark
Out of Water

Julie K. Halapchuk

iUniverse, Inc.
New York Lincoln Shanghai

A Shark Out of Water

iUniverse books may be ordered through booksellers or by contacting:

iUniverse
2021 Pine Lake Road, Suite 100
Lincoln, NE 68512
www.iuniverse.com
1-800-Authors (1-800-288-4677)

ISBN-13: 978-0-595-36122-9 (pbk)
ISBN-13: 978-0-595-80566-2 (ebk)
ISBN-10: 0-595-36122-6 (pbk)
ISBN-10: 0-595-80566-3 (ebk)

Printed in the United States of America

For Nicholas and Rachel who inspire me.

Chapter 1

Like many other sixth graders in his neighborhood, Samuel Joseph Richardson awaited the arrival of the school bus with mortal dread. The late August morning air felt fresh and warm so it didn't seem fair that he would soon be trapped in a stuffy classroom with no chance for escape until the school year ended 180 days later. He rubbed the top of his spiky, brown hair hoping to erase the cowlick that always formed near the top of his forehead. Then he looked toward the end of the street for what must have been the thirtieth time and still saw no sign of the large yellow vehicle of doom that would transport him to school.

The morning had started off with a bang with his sixteen-year-old sister, Stacy, screaming at him to exit the bathroom so she could finish applying two layers of makeup before leaving the house. He found her obsession with her face, hair and clothes to be bizarre since he would be comfortable wearing the same clothes and not touching a bar of soap for at least 3 days—possibly 4 days in the winter. He typically stayed an extra long time in the bathroom when she acted this way. He really didn't do anything in there except make faces in front of the mirror and laugh at Stacy until Mom ended the standoff.

The battle continued in the kitchen as Sammy used the last drop of milk in the house before Stacy had an opportunity to pour her cereal. Could he have saved her some milk? Certainly. But it was just too fun to watch her have a tantrum, and he usually knew just what to do to make her angry. Little brothers have an uncanny sense about these things. Of course, Sammy and Stacy also had a younger sister, Selma, and Sammy had learned very quickly that two-year-old sisters know just how to get on your nerves, too.

Surprisingly, Stacy had calmed down before she left the house that morning and actually wished Sammy good luck at school. Sammy smiled and wished her the same, feeling bad about what he had done earlier—for at least a few seconds. Even though they fought daily, Sammy knew his sister was worried about him today. This was his first day at a new school after having moved to a new town in Pennsylvania over the summer. Scary stuff!

Sammy pushed his glasses further up his nose, wiped his brow and looked down the street again. Maybe the bus driver didn't know he had moved to Springdale and wasn't planning on picking him up today. What would happen then? Perhaps he could homeschool himself. Let's see, if he counted all of his trading cards then that would be a good math lesson. He also wondered if he could some-how play video games and translate that into something educa-tional. He thought for a minute that maybe he should go back in the house and tell Mom that he'd like her to be his teacher. It might be easier than meeting so many new people in one day.

Their house that seemed so strange to him not long ago now looked comforting in the late summer sun. The yellow siding that once looked gross to him was now friendly and inviting. And his fam-ily's welcome sign that featured a colorful butterfly was now beck-oning to him to return to his room and eat chocolate chip cookies until he almost burst. If he stayed home, he could daydream about places far away, watch television until his eyes crossed and never worry about what other people thought of him.

He missed the friends he had made at his old school. He was comfortable there in a way that he wasn't sure he could be in this new place. Springdale was nice enough. He liked the park down the hill from their house and the nearby museums, movie theater and bowling alley. And he had discovered the best ice cream in the world just down the street—his favorite was a strange yet excellent mix of banana, chocolate and black raspberry. But there really weren't any boys his age that lived on his street, and his family had spent a lot of time in the house unpacking after they moved so he felt like he really didn't know anyone here yet.

But his biggest concern was that the kids at school would make fun of him. He had grown up with the kids in his old hometown so they knew very early on that he had been born with a birth defect called Spina Bifida. His mom had even arranged for someone to come to his class and talk about what Spina Bifida was so they would feel more comfortable with Sammy. She offered to do the same at his new school, but he was very nervous that this would put a spotlight on how different he was from the other kids. He didn't think that was a good idea right now.

As he continued to wait for the bus, he looked down at his legs that were covered with white braces and strips of velcro that held his legs inside of them. Perhaps he should have worn pants instead of shorts, but he decided that the kids would notice that he swayed a bit when he walked anyway so it wouldn't matter. He also knew they would soon notice that he missed school quite a bit for doctor appointments and surgeries, and that he visited the nurse at least once a day for medication or other problems. Finally, he was sure they would figure out that he often needed extra help and time in learning the same things they were learning in the classroom. If only he could focus on his schoolwork for long periods of time, he would be a straight A student. Instead, he often started a task then lost interest and began to think about anything other than school.

When he was feeling particularly unfocused, usually in math class, he would doodle on his notebook or fidget in his chair. No matter how much he tried, the numbers would swirl around in his head making no sense at all. Usually if his teacher was patient and stopped by his desk to explain what he should be doing again, he would go back to his work. But would his teachers at the new school help him or think he was being difficult? He didn't mean to get bored. It just happened. He was getting older now and his parents lectured him endlessly about being responsible. Maybe they were throwing him to the wolves now.

Sammy was still deep in thought when the bus pulled up to the curb just in front of their house. He looked back at his house long-ingly and thought he saw his mother peeking out from behind a cur-tain. Sammy had warned Mom not to walk him to the bus, and he could have sworn that Dad had to put Mom on a leash to restrain her from running out there and kissing him goodbye. Aren't parents scary?

The foldable bus door opened and a middle-aged lady with a baseball cap stating that "Grandmas Rock" looked down at Sammy, "All aboard, young man. I'm Joanie, and you must be the new kid on the block."

Sammy winced at her comment about being the new kid and said, "I'm Sammy."

"Well, Sam, welcome to your first day at Springdale Middle School," Joanie said with a wink and a grin.

Sammy climbed aboard and walked to his seat. He noticed a few of the kids glancing and sometimes staring hard at his legs. He sat down in the fourth seat from the front and hugged his bright red bookbag to his chest. He began to stare out the window as the bus moved toward its destination certain that he would throw up at any minute.

The ride was unusually quiet although he heard whispers coming from the back of the bus and was sure that some of the kids were talking about him. He tried not to let it bother him, but his hair was now standing at attention on the back of his neck. Mom always said that kids are curious, but once they get to know you, they don't even notice the leg braces. For the most part, he thought she was right, but that never made meeting new classmates any easier.

The bus lurched to a halt in front of the yellow brick school, and Joanie announced, "Have a great day, guys!"

Joanie's passengers slowly climbed down the steps of the bus and embarked on their new year at school. Sammy was the last to leave his seat, and Joanie could tell that he was nervous. As he walked past her, she said, "Don't forget that you're on Bus 101. And don't forget to have fun today."

"Thanks," Sammy replied without looking at her. He felt like looking at anyone might make him cry.

Chapter 2

With his backpack in tow, Sammy walked toward the double front doors of the school. The building looked enormous. He could feel sweat pouring down the sides of his face near his hairline now, and he hoped no one would notice. As he placed his hand on the handle of the door on the right, Sammy felt a tap on his left shoulder.

"Hey, is your name Sam?" asked a tall boy with jet black hair.

"Yes."

"What happened to your legs?" the tall boy asked.

The question made Sammy feel as if he'd been punched in the stomach. He knew that he should expect these questions, but he still wasn't ready for them. He thought it might be great if he could think of a witty reply, but nothing occurred to him.

"Oh...Um...I was born with something that made my leg muscles weak. Doesn't really go away. The braces help me walk better," answered Sammy reluctantly.

"Oh, okay. What grade are you in, Sam?

"Sixth."

"Me, too. I'm Andrew. Do you know where to go?" he asked as if concerned that Sammy might walk into the building and be lost forever amongst old books and gym equipment.

Sammy smiled and answered now realizing that Andrew was not going to be an enemy, but possibly a friend, "I'm supposed to check in at the office first. Do you know where that is?"

"Sure," said Andrew, "It's right through this door and on the right. The secretary will help you. You'll probably be assigned to a homeroom first."

"I got a letter in the mail that said I've been assigned to Mrs. Dawson's homeroom," said Sammy.

"Me, too! I'll wait for you then we can walk to homeroom together," Andrew offered as they entered the office.

"Thanks, but how did you know my name?"

"Small town…and my mom is a real estate agent so she knows about everyone who's moving in."

Sammy quickly checked in with the school secretary, and then he and Andrew were on their way to Mrs. Dawson's class. Tall, quick Andrew and short Sammy walked down the crowded hall together. Even though Sammy was in a new environment, he realized that Andrew had already made him feel comfortable.

"Here it is. I guess we can just sit anywhere until Mrs. Dawson comes in and tells us what to do," said Andrew.

"Great," said Sammy entering the already crowded room reluctantly.

Sensing that Sam was nervous, Andrew tried to distract him with small talk, "So what kind of stuff do you like to do?" asked Andrew.

"I like football and baseball," Sammy replied, "And I collect comic books."

"Hey, I collect comic books, too! Have you been to Jack's Collectibles in town?" Andrew asked.

"No. Do they have some good books?"

Andrew excitedly pulled three comic books from his backpack and showed them to Sammy, "You bet. Look at these babies. I just bought them last week."

"Cool," Sam gasped as he stared at Andrew's treasures.

Just then Mrs. Dawson entered the room. She had a look on her face that made Sammy think she might be really tired of teaching. Sammy thought she could be about his grandmother's age so she might be nearing retirement. Andrew quickly pulled the comic books from Sammy's hands and returned them to his backpack before Mrs. Dawson would have a chance to confiscate them.

Mrs. Dawson looked over the rims of her thick glasses and said, "Good morning, class."

A few students half-heartedly said, "Good morning, Mrs. Dawson."

Moving in front of her desk, Mrs. Dawson grinned, "I can tell by that response that all of you are excited to be back here for another year."

A few giggles emerged from the back of the classroom. Sammy, who had taken a seat very close to the front of the room, began to squirm uncomfortably there. Where was this going? Mrs. Dawson seemed like the type who might give you detention just for looking at her the wrong way. He sat in his chair quietly trying to fly below her radar. No such luck.

"Everyone—we have a new student at our school this year. Please give a warm welcome to Samuel Richardson," she said pointing at Sammy, "Would you like to introduce yourself?"

Sammy blushed as he stood up next to his desk, "I'm Sammy. I just moved here a few weeks ago with my parents and two sisters."

"Are your sisters cute?" yelled a freckle-faced boy from the back of the room as all the students laughed.

"Well, one of them is sixteen, but you might like the other one better. She's two years old," Sammy shot back, but knew that sarcasm was probably not the best idea on the first day at a new school.

"Harsh...but funny," Andrew said loudly.

"That'll be enough boys," Mrs. Dawson said looking like she regretted introducing Sammy to the class, "Let's learn about the rules of our classroom now."

It seemed to Sammy that Mrs. Dawson went on to recite about five thousand rules for the classroom. He was sweating again at the prospect that maybe he shouldn't have been such a "smartie pants" with the freckle-faced boy. The class and the rest of the morning dragged on.

Chapter 3

By lunchtime Sammy was exhausted. He was bored with introducing himself again and again and just wished there were one person at school that he already knew. It would be good to go back home and see his friends who already knew what his favorite sports and movies were.

In the cafeteria, there were a ton of kids. He didn't see Andrew anywhere so he sat alone at a table in the far corner of the cafeteria by the garbage can. This was a big mistake. One by one as the kids came up to throw out their leftover food and paper products, they would stare at Sammy. Sometimes they only looked at the braces on his legs without even bothering to look at his face. Others acknowledged him quietly.

Then someone who you wouldn't want to acknowledge you stopped over. His name was Derek, and he seemed bigger than any sixth grader that Sammy had ever seen. Classic bully.

"What's your name?" asked Derek.

"Sam."

"Hmmm. I don't know if I want to call you by your real name, or if I want to make up some embarrassing nickname that you'll hate. Let me think about that for a while," snickered Derek.

Sammy couldn't say anything. He was speechless at Derek's complete honesty. A million nicknames that he would not want to be called swirled through his head as he looked at Derek to see what else was coming out of his mouth.

"So what's with the casts on your legs?" Derek asked.

"They're not casts. They're braces. They just help me walk better," Sammy explained sensing that he had provided too much information, which would become ammunition for someone like Derek.

"Really? I guess you can't run around like everybody else," said Derek nastily.

"I walk fast."

"Well, you'll have to show me in gym class. Wow—how are you going to take gym?" asked Derek who looked like he might laugh at any moment.

"Don't worry. I'll get by," retorted Sammy.

Derek responded with the cruel words he hadn't wanted to hear, "You are different. A bit of a freak, I guess."

As Derek waited for a reply, Sammy thought that his old school was nicer because at least he knew who his enemies were there. Now he had to learn who to stay away from and who might become a friend all over again. It was like guerilla warfare in middle school. The school bell rang with perfect timing, and Sammy did not have to respond to Derek's last vicious comment. Sammy was sure he would run into Derek many more times this year.

After lunch, Sammy went on to math, science and social studies classes. Even though he really didn't like math, he was happy when he saw that Andrew was in that class with him. And the math teacher, Mrs. Dietrich, was his favorite teacher by far. She was very sweet and really explained what she needed the students to do in a way that he could easily understand.

The afternoon moved slowly, but finally the school day had ended. He couldn't believe he was getting anxious to go home and complain to his mother about the horrors of school. Hopefully, the bus ride home would be uneventful without any 'Dereks' onboard.

Just as Sammy prepared to board the bus for the ride home, he looked to his right and saw a student he hadn't yet met. To his surprise, the boy was in a wheelchair and actually looked somewhat like Sammy with the same messy brown hair and tiny build. But, this boy didn't have glasses like Sammy did.

Sammy thought that maybe he could connect with this guy. At least this person would know what it's like to be different. It excited Sammy that someone else in his school had a disability. At his last school, he was the only student who had one.

"Hey! I'm Sammy—new kid," Sammy introduced himself nervously.

The boy smiled, "Yeah. I heard you were here today."

"What?"

"A friend of mine who plays wheelchair basketball with me said there was another kid at school with a disability. I figured it had to be you," he said pointing at Sammy's braces.

Sammy asked, "What's your name?"

The boy grinned, "I'm Nick. I'm in sixth grade."

"Me, too," said Sammy.

"You just gotta get used to being at a new school," said Nick who sensed that Sammy must've had a hard day, "Some of the kids are pretty cool once you get to know them."

"I guess."

"Did you have the pleasure of meeting Derek yet?" asked Nick sarcastically.

Sammy sighed, "At lunch today. He called me a freak."

Nick laughed, "That's so original. He should think of something new because he used to call me that, too."

"Really?"

"Just give it some time. Not everyone is like Derek," Nick decided to change the subject, "Are you riding the bus today?"

"Sure. Are you?"

"No. My mom picks me up. It's a pain to try to get a special bus to take my wheelchair and me," Nick replied, "Plus I like to get home and watch my favorite shows before I have to do homework."

Just then Joanie the bus driver signaled to Sammy to get on the bus. Sammy waved goodbye to Nick and climbed up the steps of the bus. The day was tough and long so he was exhausted, but now it seemed a little better since he had talked to Nick.

Chapter 4

The bus ride home was relatively quiet. In fact it was uneventful. Sammy was thankful for that because it gave him a chance to think over everything that had happened that day. It seemed like it had been a month since he had seen his home and family. He was looking forward to talking to his parents and even to Stacy.

As Sammy left the bus, he waved goodbye to Joanie and saw his Mom waiting at the front door. When was Mom going to get the hint that an 11-year-old boy does not want his mother to greet him when he gets off of the school bus? He was afraid to look back at the kids who remained on the bus because they might be doubling over with laughter and calling him a mama's boy or some other fun nickname that could stick to him for the rest of his life. How embarrassing! But what a relief it was to see a familiar face.

"How was school today?" Mom asked as they walked to the kitchen, and she fixed him a snack.

"I really hated it most of the day. The classes were boring and there was hardly anybody to talk to. Plus my homeroom teacher is mega cranky...but I did meet two kids that I liked," Sammy paused to take a breath.

"Well you always say that school is boring and at least one teacher is cranky every year. They usually end up being your favorite teachers after a while," Mom reminded him, "Tell me about the kids you met."

"Their names are Andrew and Nick. They are both sixth graders. Andrew likes comic books. He told me about a place in town that sells some awesome ones. I didn't get to talk to Nick for a long time because I met him at the end of the day when I was going to catch my bus. I know he plays wheelchair basketball though."

Mom smiled, "See—you have a lot in common with those boys. If you want, I could take you and Andrew to the comic book store sometime. Maybe he or Nick would like to come over and play sometime, too."

Sammy rolled his eyes in disgust, "Mom, sixth graders don't play."

"Really?" she replied with a stunned look.

"We hang out," Sammy said as he chomped on a huge chocolate chip cookie.

"My mistake," Mom laughed, "You know, it must be nice to have someone else at school who is physically challenged. Nick can probably relate to a lot of the same issues that you can."

"We'll see. I only just met him, but he seems nice. He's probably more like me than everyone else," said Sammy.

"Sam, you never know how much you have in common with other people until you get to know them. Now, I know you are sick of hearing that from me, but it really is true. Everyone has some kind of challenge," Mom said.

"I got it. I got it. That's the same lecture you've given me for about fifty years now!" Sammy rolled his eyes.

Mom snapped him in the leg with a dishtowel and laughed, "Get your sister. I haven't heard a peep out of her, and I want to find out how her day was, too."

As soon as Sammy called for Stacy, she descended the stairs carrying Selma who had managed to find Stacy's jewelry and makeup—again. Selma's face seemed to have all of the colors of the rainbow on it, and she had so many necklaces around her neck that she jingled. Her face lit up when she saw the cookies on their kitchen table.

"Stacy, tell me about your day," Mom said as she began to chop vegetables for dinner.

Stacy beamed, "It was awesome! There are an absolute ton of after-school activities and clubs to join. And believe it or not, the cafeteria actually has a salad bar instead of all that vending machine and greasy stuff we had at our old school. But the best thing of all is that there are some really hot guys in my class. The absolute hottest is Trevor and he already talked to me twice. I want him to ask me to the Homecoming dance."

"Isn't that a month or two away?" Mom asked.

"Are you sure that's enough time to decide what to wear?" Sammy joked.

"What a clown," Stacy deadpanned, "The dance is in October so there is plenty of time to get to know Trevor! There are so many more social activities in this school than in my last one."

"Well, let's keep the number of activities to a minimum. I'm not driving you to ten different activities, and you are not borrowing the minivan every day," Mom replied.

"But I already decided to join at least three clubs—French, Pep and Photography."

Mom looked like she might burst a blood vessel at any minute, but calmly asked, "Stacy, why are you joining the Photography Club? Do you even own a camera?"

"No. I guess I'll need to get one. In fact, I have a whole list of stuff I'm going to need including some new shoes. Do you want to go to the mall after dinner?"

"Wow. Stacy doesn't usually have any good ideas, but as long as we're shopping can I get that new video game I wanted or go to the comic book store that Andrew told me about?" Sammy asked.

"I don't think we need to run out and spend all of our money in one night."

"Okay, but I just don't want to be unpopular simply because of an early poor shoe choice," Stacy smiled sweetly knowing that this statement might send Mom over the edge.

"I'm thinking maybe we'll drive to the mall after you get a job," Mom returned Stacy's sweet smile, "And Samuel Joseph, you need another video game or comic book like you need a hole in the head."

"We get it. We get it," Stacy grumbled and began setting the table for dinner as Sammy snickered and Selma began to play with

the dog's water dish. At least she wasn't drinking out of it this time—
yet.

Chapter 5

Later that night after Sammy had taken his bath and brushed his teeth—vigorously, of course, he lay on his bed and stared at his bedroom ceiling. Not ready to sleep yet, he looked at the stars above. Naturally, they weren't real stars, but glow in the dark ones that his parents had put there to remind him of his room at their old house. When he was in first grade, he had become interested in the sun, moon and stars so Dad had told him they should buy some at the store—ones that they could attach to his ceiling. Back then he thought that idea was the greatest one he had ever heard.

Thinking about the old house and that first day with his very own solar system made him smile. At first he thought it would be childish to keep the stars with him in the new house, but now they comforted him. He crossed his arms behind his neck and sighed as he revisited everything that had happened that day and wondered whether or not the 179 remaining days of school would pass so slowly.

"Sam," Stacy called to him as she quickly knocked on his bedroom door, "Can I come in?"

"Why?"

"C'mon, Sam. Gimme a break. I want to talk to you."

Sammy frowned, "Sure. C'mon in."

Stacy glided into the room with a pale green cream covering her face and her hair in a ponytail. She pulled up a chair and adjusted her bright pink robe before seeing his look of terror, "Very funny. You can just knock that goofy look off of your face right now. I'm giving myself a facial. So get over it."

"Do you really have to come in here looking like that now? I'm gonna have nightmares," he responded.

She snickered, "I can give you a facial if you like. It's very relaxing."

"No way. That stuff looks toxic."

"So...ready for school tomorrow?" Stacy changed the subject.

Sammy was still staring at her with dismay, "Sure."

Stacy continued with her line of questioning, "Mom told me you met a couple of new friends."

"Yep," Sammy replied just hoping Stacy would leave the room and cease with the quizzes.

"Did anything else good happen?"

"Not really. What are you getting at?" Sam asked gruffly.

Stacy lost her patience and stood up to leave the room, "Good grief. I'm just trying to check in with you and see how things are going! I swear, you clam up whenever anybody tries to ask you anything. Forget I asked, dork."

"Who are you calling a dork, princess pukeface?"

"What a jerk!" Stacy shouted and opened the door only to find Mom standing there with a look of concern on her face.

"What's going on?" Mom asked.

"Nothing," they answered in unison.

"Right. I can hear you guys clear down the hall," Mom replied, "You know, Sam, it sounded like Stacy was just trying to find out if everything is okay with you."

"Everything's fine. Why does she care?" Sam asked.

"Because she's your sister and she loves you," Mom said as she came into the room and sat down on his bed.

"Gross," Sammy and Stacy said then giggled because they were thinking the same thing.

Mom laughed, "Okay. So you tolerate each other. Sam, sometimes it isn't a bad idea to talk with your sister about school stuff. She was in sixth grade not long ago, you know."

"Right," said Stacy, "Mom and Dad went to school in the Stone Age so how can they possibly give you advice that will work for you now? That's why you should listen to me about everything instead."

"I wouldn't go that far, Sammy," Mom laughed and stood up to leave the room, "Let's wrap this up soon, guys. We have another early morning ahead of us. And Samuel, I would like you to clean your room tomorrow. I'm not sure what I just sat on that was under the quilt on your bed, but it might have been alive!"

Stacy and Sammy broke into giggles again as they heard Mom stroll down the hallway to answer Selma's bellows. Selma had a habit of screaming for a good hour before she finally settled down in her toddler bed each night. She often came out of her room five or six times within that hour. She would ask for a drink then ask someone to read her a story then ask for another drink and so on. Their parents had probably not had a full night's sleep in two years.

Stacy looked down at Sammy again, "Just let me know if you want to talk about anything. I'm right down the hall, you know."

As Stacy opened the door, Sammy replied in what might have been a moment of weakness, "Well...maybe I do have one thing we could talk about."

Sammy proceeded to tell Stacy about his school day and ask her more than one question about school and friends and even girls. It was as if the floodgates had opened. He wasn't sure why he was feeling comfortable talking with his sister about all of this stuff, but he felt better once he had. He thought that if she ever tried to blackmail him she would have a lot of ammunition, but right now he didn't care. Suddenly, Stacy was like his own personal therapist. She sat at the edge of his bed and nodded as he talked for close to an hour before Mom knocked on his door and again reminded them to go to bed.

"Goodnight, Sam. I'm glad we talked," said Stacy.

"Are you going to tell anyone what we talked about?" Sammy asked nervously.

"I was thinking of e-mailing everyone at my school," Stacy answered dryly as she patted her face and noticed that her creamy green facial mask had now dried and cracked because she had left it on her face too long.

"Huh?" Sammy said not knowing how to respond.

Stacy smiled, "Don't be ridiculous. Of course, I won't tell anyone. My lips are sealed."

"Can I still call you princess pukeface?"

"Don't push your luck," Stacy said as she picked up a pillow and threw it at him, "Goodnight, annoying brother."

"Whatever," he said rolling his eyes, "By the way, it looks like your face might be permanently green now."

After Stacy left his room, Sammy still couldn't sleep so he read one of his favorite comic books by flashlight underneath the quilt his grandmother had made him years ago. Lately he had been having trouble sleeping and tonight was no exception. He figured it was just nervousness and hoped his insomnia would end soon. This scene repeated itself again and again as the school year went on.

Chapter 6

The first few months of school seemed to fly by and before they knew it, November had rolled around. By this time the Homecoming dance had come and gone, but Trevor hadn't asked Stacy to go as his date. She was depressed about this until she realized that maybe she could snag him for the Christmas dance or spring semi-formal. Frankly, Sammy and his entire family were sick of hearing about Trevor already, and they had never met him.

Sammy was getting to know everyone at his school and had become good friends with Andrew and Nick. The boys were excited that soon they'd be away from school for a week for the Thanksgiving holiday. Any break from the monotony of homework would be welcome.

"What do you guys do over Thanksgiving break?" Sammy asked one day as they headed from the lunchroom to their next class.

Andrew answered first as he threw away his cheese sandwich because it was just entirely too gross, "We travel to my grandma's house in Harrisburg. We'll be gone for the whole break."

"We bounce between like seven different houses, and we see every aunt, uncle and cousin in the family!" laughed Nick, "How about you, Sam?"

"Dad's sister and her family live in West Virginia. We're going to visit them. My cousins are pretty cool, and we haven't seen them in a long time so it should be fun."

As the boys reached the main hallway of the school, they noticed another sixth grader posting a flyer on the school bulletin board. In no hurry to get to class, they stopped to read it. It said:

Attention: Springdale Middle School Students

Tryouts for the Springdale Sharks Sled Hockey Team will be held on December 1st immediately after school at the SuperStar Ice Rink.

Equipment will be provided.

Sled hockey is a new sport available at Springdale Middle School beginning this January. Sled hockey players play ice hockey on sleds instead of skates.

All physically challenged students are invited to be a part of the team. Two able-bodied players will also be chosen to play.

For more information, contact the school office.

"I've never heard of that sport before," Sammy said after he finished reading the flyer.

"Me neither," said Andrew.

Nick was still staring at the flyer as he spoke, "I saw it played once on TV during the Paralympics."

"What's that?" asked Andrew.

"It's like the Olympics except people with disabilities play," said Nick, "I think they usually play the Paralympics every four years just like the Olympics. There are other sports, too, like adapted skiing and stuff like that."

"Hmmm," said Sammy, "Do you think we should go to the try-outs?"

"Sure," cheered Nick who always seemed to be the bravest of the three and always the first to try new things.

"Are you in, Andrew?" asked Sammy.

Just then Sammy noticed that Andrew looked a little uncomfortable with the conversation they'd been having. Andrew shuffled a bit and said, "I don't think that sport is meant for me."

Nick read the bottom of the flyer out loud, "Two able-bodied players will also be chosen to play."

Sammy said, "Nick, maybe Andrew doesn't want to play since almost everyone on the team will have a disability and he doesn't."

"That's not true, Sam," answered Andrew, "I was just thinking it would be neat to try out, but what if I really stink? I've never played sled hockey."

Nick laughed, "Neither have we. We can look like total geeks together."

"Are you in?" asked Sammy.

"Yeah, I'll try it," said Andrew, "It can't be any worse than how bad I am at golf."

"Or science!" laughed Sammy.

"Yeah, or at playing volleyball," said Nick.

Andrew frowned, "Okay, you guys. I get the picture. You don't think I'm good at anything."

Sammy elbowed him, "We're kidding and you know it. You're an awesome comic book collector and a soccer star."

"Well, maybe not a star—but definitely gifted!" Andrew exclaimed then ran into his class as he heard the bell ring. Nick and Sammy picked up their pace now, making it to their classes just in time for the second bell to ring. Thankful he wasn't tardy, Sammy opened his book and tried to pay attention to the teacher instead of thinking about sled hockey.

The rest of the day was spent talking about the upcoming holiday and the sled hockey tryouts every time he saw Nick and Andrew. Sammy couldn't wait to tell his parents—and maybe even his older sister—about the tryouts. November was turning out to be his most awesome month in Springdale.

Chapter 7

Sammy told his entire family about the tryouts over Thanksgiving break at his Aunt Ann's house. He had never seen the sport played, but was just excited that he, Andrew and Nick might be on a team together. Andrew already played soccer, and Nick played wheelchair basketball, but Sammy didn't play on a team at all.

"So what position do you think you'd like to play?" Stacy asked Sammy while pulling the disgusting and somewhat burnt skin off of her piece of Thanksgiving Day turkey. It was no secret that Aunt Ann could not cook very well, but this year's meal was especially scary. Stacy was tempted to throw one of the hot rolls at Sammy for kicks, but she thought he might get a concussion because they were so hard.

Dad chimed in since the talk had turned to sports—his absolute favorite subject, "Well, the coach might evaluate Sammy and his friends then decide where he thinks they should play."

Stacy frowned, "You mean, you don't get a choice? What ever happened to freedom of choice in Springdale?"

Mom laughed, "Calm down, Ms. Protestor. From what I've seen, you choose to not clean your room pretty regularly. And, of course, I am free to ground you!"

Everyone laughed at that little joke except for Stacy. She was tired of doing chores and happy not to think about them while they went about visiting family over the break. It would be a shame to go back to the old dungeon once their trip was over.

"Well, here's an FYI for you guys—Selma raids my room like every day so even when it starts out clean, it doesn't stay that way. I think you should try punishing her for once," Stacy pointed to Selma who was currently rolling peas off of her plate, down the side of the table and into the open mouth of Aunt Ann's dog.

Mom stopped Selma's pea-rolling activity and changed the subject fearing that a teenage or possibly even a toddler tantrum was just around the corner, "Sammy, would it be okay if I went to the try-outs with you?"

"Oh, Mom. Are you kidding?"

"No. I have to drive you there anyway, right? I just want to sit in the stands and watch," Mom replied, "It sounds interesting."

"I wouldn't mind going either. I could drive Sam," Stacy said nonchalantly.

"Good grief. I'd like to get there in one piece. I've seen the way you drive, and it scares me," said Sammy, "Mom, you can drive me. And you guys can go, but do not yell my name or do anything to embarrass me in any way."

"No problem," Stacy grinned mischieviously.

"Do you solemnly swear on your super cool hairstyle that you won't embarrass me?" Sammy screeched.

Stacy put her hand on her chest, closed her eyes and solemnly swore that she would let Sammy give her a buzz cut if she embarrassed him. Stacy didn't think she looked good with short hair so she certainly didn't think she'd look good with no hair! She was pretty sure that she wouldn't say a word during tryouts.

Aunt Ann sensed that they were ending their little ceremony. She stood up and asked, "Does anyone want pumpkin pie now?"

Everyone groaned at the thought of one more bite of food. Of course, two hours later they were all back in the kitchen scrambling for a piece of pie, which was surprisingly good. Stacy had to admit that Thanksgiving was one of her favorite holidays. She liked getting together with the whole family, playing football in the front yard in a fashionable autumn outfit and shopping on Black Friday, which kicked off the holiday shopping season. Sammy loved it, too, except for Aunt Ann's cooking.

Stacy felt so good that she decided to peek in on Sammy before they went to bed, "Sam, do you have to wear anything special to the sled hockey tryouts?"

Sammy looked up from the cartoon he was watching, "The flyer didn't say we had to wear anything special. Why?"

"I was just wondering because I know that the ice rink has practice jerseys for sale in their shop. If you want, I could buy one for you. Consider it an early Christmas present," she offered.

"Why?" he asked again suspiciously.

"Just because I have to get you a gift anyway or Mom and Dad will punish me forever. So I might as well get you something you need."

Sammy smiled, "You aren't starting to like me are you?"

"Not a chance. Besides fulfilling my obligation to give you a gift, you would also look more like a real hockey player. I mean, if you would actually start dressing a little better, I might tell people that you are my brother," Stacy added.

"What do you tell people now?"

Stacy rolled her eyes, laughed and walked toward the door, "Sometimes I tell them you are our foreign exchange student. Most of the time I pretend I don't know you at all."

Stacy felt something hit the middle of her back. Luckily, it was only a pillow. She popped in on Selma to find her fast asleep with her favorite stuffed bunny rabbit. Then she scooted down the hallway to share a room with her cousin. There she planned on dreaming sweet dreams of their shopping trip the next day.

While Stacy dreamed about clothes and shoes, Sammy dreamed that he was a sled hockey player and that he scored a winning goal, which made everyone in the crowd stand up and cheer. Then the mayor of Springdale gave him the key to the city and held a parade in his honor. What a great dream!

Chapter 8

The first day of December finally rolled around and Andrew, Nick and Sammy rode to the SuperStar Ice Rink with Sammy's family. The ride was short since the rink was only a mile away from school. Sammy was surprised at the number of cars in the parking lot and got a little nervous at the thought of possibly trying out in front of a large crowd.

Sammy and his friends soon found out they didn't need to worry about a crowd. Since there were three separate rinks in the SuperStar Ice Rink, three times as many hockey players could be in the building at any time. Today, all of the rinks were being used, but for the sled hockey tryouts, there weren't a lot of onlookers—mostly the potential players and their parents.

Dad, who had taken a vacation day from work to be at the tryouts, opened the double doors to Rink #1. Sammy was happy that Dad was with them since he was the one person in their family who truly appreciated sports. Mom and Stacy were clueless about most sports, and Selma was too young to care. Sammy entered the rink first and felt a cold rush of air on his face. He must have looked confused about where to go because a man holding a clipboard approached him.

"Are any of you here to try out for the team?" the man asked.

Sammy pointed to himself and his friends, "Yes, we wanted to check it out. Are you the coach?"

"No. I'm an assistant coach. My name is Joel," he said handing his clipboard to Sammy, "Each player needs to sign in. The coach will come over to talk with everyone in a minute."

As the boys talked with Joel, Sammy's family sat down on the bleachers. Stacy exclaimed, "Woo! These are cold!"

"I know," Mom laughed, "I'm not sure if I'm going to like this sport too much. We're going to freeze our butts off."

"Yeah! Why can't Sammy play a sport that involves lying out at the beach? Now that's a sport I could get into," said Stacy.

Of course, Selma was having a grand old time already. She loved jumping up and down the metal stairs because they made so much noise. And the ramp by the bleachers was a perfect runway for her. She took off like a plane and ran so fast that Stacy thought she wouldn't stop, and they'd be scraping her off of the cement wall.

While he talked with his friends, Sammy watched Mom trying her best to slow Selma down and rolled his eyes. He also noticed Stacy gawking at all of the hockey players that were now stopping over at Rink #1 to see what was going on with the sled hockey tryouts. He should have known she would be here on a boyfriend hunt and not to watch him play. He decided to pull some kind of prank or do something that would torture her later that night.

Nick noticed Sammy watching all of the activity going on with his family, "Your sisters are crazy, Sam."

"Tell me about it. And I have to live with them!" Sammy exclaimed.

Andrew interrupted, "Did you guys see some of the girls who are here to try out?"

"Sure. So what?" Nick asked as he dug into the pocket of his jeans for some gum that he then offered the boys.

"Just wondered if you saw them," Andrew replied.

Chewing feverishly and blowing a monstrous bubble, Nick then snickered and elbowed Sammy, "I think Andrew might be in love."

Sammy started giggling as Andrew blushed. Sammy had also noticed that there were a few girls his age at the rink now. It hadn't occurred to him that girls would want to play sled hockey. One of the girls there was Madeline Ryan. She happened to sit in front of him in his English class, and he thought she was pretty cute. As weird as it sounded, his favorite thing about her was that she always smelled good. He also liked her long, red hair that she often braided or pulled back with a large brown barrette.

Andrew protested, "No. I just don't want to look like a geek in front of them. I didn't think girls would try out."

Nick answered matter-of-factly, "Well, no one said they couldn't. Sam, what's up with you and Madeline?"

Sammy exclaimed, "What do you mean?"

Nick, who was keenly observant and always willing to state his opinion, said, "C'mon. You're staring at her. And I know she's in one of your classes."

"Yeah. She's in my English class. I just recognized her, that's all."

"Right," said Nick.

"Okay. Okay. She's cute. But I don't know if I want to play sports with her. I'm probably going to stink at first. Possibly forever," replied Sammy.

"Man, I know what you mean," Andrew exclaimed, "Not everyone is confident like you are, Nick."

Nick laughed, "My mom says I'm not so much confident as stubborn. I just don't like it when somebody tells me I can't do something."

The boys continued to chat then they saw that their wait to learn more about sled hockey was coming to an end as Joel began walking over to the crowd. He signaled for everyone to quiet down. They were excited and nervous at the same time, and Sammy was also having trouble focusing since Madeline was now only a few feet away from where he stood. He was surprised when she smiled shyly and waved to him. He guessed he had been staring at her a little too much.

Chapter 9

"Hi, everyone. My name is Joel and I'd like to welcome you to the Springdale Sharks sled hockey tryouts. I'm the assistant coach, and I'm glad to see we've had such a good turnout today," said Joel, "I'd like to introduce the coach of our team, Rachel Michaels."

Sammy's family could see Sammy's jaw drop from where they were seated. He and his friends all looked at each other in surprise. Their coach was a female? Sam figured they might play with a few girls, but their coach was a girl? That hadn't even occurred to him.

Coach Rachel smiled at the boys as if she knew what they were thinking and thought it was amusing, "Good afternoon. I'm Coach Rachel. Thanks for coming to our first tryout. I have been a coach for a high school hockey team for the last 7 years, but I have never been as excited as I am about the opportunity to coach this team."

Everyone in the crowd clapped in support. Sammy looked around and saw about fifteen kids, including at least eight who were in wheelchairs. All of the player's faces were beaming at the prospect of being part of the team.

Coach Rachel continued, "Today we are going to let each of you try out a sled and see how you like it. Please don't be discouraged if you can't move very well on the sled at first. It takes lots of practice to move where you want, when you want in one of these contraptions!"

Assistant Coach Joel continued as he held up a pair of what looked like very short hockey sticks, "We are sure a lot of you aren't familiar with this sport so let me show you the sticks you will be using. The flat end of the stick has a pick in it, which digs into the ice. You put a stick in each hand and propel yourself like you are rowing a boat."

"The sled looks just like one that you might go sled riding on. You will be strapped into the sled with a few seat belts so you can go as fast as possible without worrying about falling out," Coach Rachel said as she pointed to one of the sleds.

"We have hockey equipment available to you. Please form a line and go over to our equipment table to see what fits you. You will need all of the same equipment that any other hockey player would use except for skates," announced Joel.

As Joel pointed to the table, the line of potential players began to form and everyone in the bleachers started chatting. Stacy noticed that the kids were of all different shapes, sizes and challenges, but they were joking and laughing as if they'd known each other forever. This seemed like it was going to be pretty cool.

"What do you think of all this, Stacy?" Dad asked.

"I was just thinking that it's pretty neat how all the kids look so different, but are acting like they've known each other forever."

Mom nodded in agreement, "Yes. It would be great if this works out for Sammy. I think he would really get a chance to make some new friends and build up his self confidence."

Dad replied, "I think they could be quite an inspiration to everyone at their school."

A few players who were already dressed were now taking to the ice. As they boarded their sleds and took hold of their shortened hockey sticks, Sammy's family finally understood what Joel and Coach Rachel had been talking about. It did look a little bit like the players were rowing a boat. But how would they hit the puck? As if he was reading their minds, Joel began to speak again about what was going on.

Joel said, "Well, now you can see how the players move on the ice. In order to move the puck along the ice, the player will need to use the opposite end of the stick to hit the puck. You can see that the other end of the stick is curved just like a regulation hockey stick."

"Wow," Mom said as she saw what Joel meant, "I wonder who thought of that!"

Stacy laughed, "I know! That's so cool."

Then they saw Sammy on the ice. He looked up to where they were sitting in the stands and waved his stick then proceeded to pass the puck to Nick. He seemed to be moving slowly, but had good aim. Selma jumped up and down as she saw him, visibly showing the excitement that the entire family felt for him.

After about 45 minutes, everyone departed the ice and returned their equipment to the table. Joel and Coach Rachel were busy looking at their clipboards and discussing what they had seen. The players looked nervous, but happy and especially very sweaty!

Coach Rachel spoke up, "Well, I'm happy to say that all fifteen players who tried out today can be a part of the team if they like. We will need some more time to determine what positions and how often each of you will play. If you'd still like to be a part of the team, we will hold practice every Thursday at 3 pm at this rink. Next week you will permanently receive your equipment including a sled, sticks and the equipment you tried on today. So, we'll see you next Thursday!"

There was a huge round of applause as Coach Rachel concluded her speech. Sammy, Andrew and Nick moved toward Sammy's family with tired, but happy faces. Selma ran to Sammy and gave him a big hug. Stacy had to maintain her big sister attitude so she refrained from hugging.

Dad patted Sammy on the back, "You guys did great out there."

"Was that wicked or what?" Andrew squealed.

"Wicked?" Dad repeated quizzically.

Sammy chimed in, "That means it was awesome, Dad. It's a lot of work, but I loved it."

"So all of you are joining the team, then?" Mom asked.

"No doubt!" exclaimed Nick.

Sammy's family had never seen three preteen boys talk as much as Sammy, Andrew and Nick did on the way out of the rink and on the ride home. Besides being excited about playing, they had received flyers from Coach Rachel about plans for the team to travel for a few games. They were really looking forward to the possibility of going on roadtrips together.

After they dropped off Andrew and Nick at their houses, Sammy was still beaming, but quieted down a little. And though it was very unlike her, Stacy turned to him and said, "You looked good out there today, Sam. I'm proud of you."

"Thanks," he replied with a smile then promptly fell asleep from exhaustion before they could pull into their driveway.

Chapter 10

The following Thursday, Mom offered to take Sammy, Andrew and Nick to their first official practice. Stacy tagged along although there was a really good sale going on at the mall. She was also missing French club, but wasn't too concerned because they never did much during club meetings anyway. Of course, she wanted to support Sammy and the boys, but just as importantly, she wanted to talk to Ben, one of the hockey players she had met the previous week while waiting in line for a snack at the rink.

After parking the minivan and scooping up Selma from her car seat, Mom elbowed Stacy and said, "I wonder if number 39 will be there today. What was his name?"

"Ben...but Mom, please do not talk about him—especially in front of these toads," Stacy said pointing to Sammy and his buddies.

"Who are you calling a toad, princess pukeface?" Sammy said as he gave Stacy a little push.

"Good one," laughed Andrew.

"Yeah. Sometimes I really wish I had a sister to torture," Nick said sadly.

Sammy smiled, "Well, since you're an only child, I'd be happy to let you torture Stacy."

"Okay, guys. Let's try to be civil and get to practice on time," Mom tried to look stern.

The rush of cold air as they entered the rink was always refreshing. The players took to the ice quickly and lined up as Coach Rachel told them about some of the drills she'd like to do to kick off practice. Sammy was having quite a hard time pushing himself along the ice, and he certainly had not perfected his turns or shots. He could feel his ears turning red with frustration.

Coach Rachel skated up to him, "Hey, Sam. How's it going?"

"Not good."

"It's okay if you don't know how to do everything at the first practice, Sam."

"I know," he said solemnly.

Coach Rachel patted him on the back, "I think we are going to call it a day now. Don't worry. You'll be getting plenty of practice before you have to play in a real game. I know a lot of players who struggled at first then went on to become great sled hockey players."

"Really?" Sammy asked.

"Honest," Coach Rachel smiled then blew her whistle, "Okay, everyone. Hit the locker rooms."

Sammy was still feeling a bit sad because he really thought he would do a better job on the sled, but he tried to be cheerful as they glided to the side of the rink to get out of their sleds. Andrew and Nick were joking around. They seemed to really be good at this sport.

The boys came off the ice soon after Sammy's Mom sat down. Mom had been helping Selma find ice and bandages during the practice due to a little injury she sustained while pretending to be an airplane on one of the ramps leading to the rink. With sweat rolling down their faces, they escaped to the locker room to put on their street clothes and generally goof around. What is it about the male species that makes them get so giddy when they enter a smelly room with no furniture?

Coach Rachel stopped to chat with Sammy's mother and sister while the boys dressed, "How are you ladies doing today?"

"Just fine. Practice seemed like it went well from what I could see," Mom replied as she pointed to Selma and her bandaged knee, "I missed a little bit of it due to an injury."

"Yes, the kids seem like they are really picking up on the rules of the game quickly. Did Joel give you the flyer with information about our little road trip?"

"Road trip?" Stacy asked, "Sammy mentioned that. Where will they go and when? And do you need like a team mascot or something?"

Coach Rachel laughed, "The good news is that the whole family is welcome to come, and you don't need to dress up like a mascot, Stacy. We're going to try to play in our first tournament in two months."

"Wow," Mom said, "Do you think they'll be ready? They've only just started playing."

"Maybe not, but it will be good experience for them. If they win, they can go to the next tournament and the next. There's also a regional championship in May," Coach Rachel said with a gleam in her eyes, "And if they don't do well, we will at least have had the chance to travel and get to know each other better."

"Where's the first tournament being held?" Stacy asked.

"Philadelphia."

"Awesome. We've never been there, Mom," Stacy said tugging on Mom's sleeve, "Can we go?"

"I don't see a reason not to. We'll make sure your Dad can take some time off of work before we say for sure."

"Well, it's time for my team pep talk," Coach Rachel laughed and knocked on both the boys' and girls' locker room doors to ask the players to come out.

After the pep talk, Sammy and his family and friends jumped in the minivan. The boys were above and beyond excited on the way home from practice. Even Sammy lightened up about how he had played and started joking around with the guys. They dropped off Nick first since he lived closest to the rink and then Andrew was next.

At home, it was back to the old grindstone. Stacy had a ton of homework, but after an hour, she seemed to only have written 'Ben' in her notebook about twenty times since she had talked with him at the rink while Sammy practiced. Sam passed by her room and noticed her goofing off.

"What are you doing, weirdo?" he asked.

"Why are you staring into my room?" Stacy shot back.

"I just noticed you not doing anything—including your homework," Sam replied.

"So you're going to Philly to play sled hockey, huh?" Stacy said changing the subject.

"I guess. If we're ready."

Stacy laughed, "You'd better get ready. I want to take a road trip."

"Whatever," he rolled his eyes, "You'd better get back to writing that guy's name in your notebook."

Chapter 11

Sammy and his new teammates practiced for a few more weeks before Christmas break. Then Coach Rachel arranged for everyone to get together for a holiday party at a nearby restaurant and entertainment center. The place was awesome according to Sammy and his friends because it featured great pizza and some of the best video games they could find within a 50-mile radius.

As they chomped on their dinner, Coach Rachel stood up to make an announcement, "I'd like to thank all of the players and families for coming out to play with us tonight. I'm really happy with the progress you've made in these past few weeks."

Everyone clapped and began chanting, "Go Sharks! Go Sharks!"

"Okay. Calm down," Coach Rachel smiled, "As I was saying, I'm proud of you so I decided that you all deserved a little holiday gift."

The clapping began again, this time more feverishly. Coach Rachel saw that it would probably be a waste of time to try to quiet everyone down so she signaled to Joel to begin handing out boxes that were wrapped in green foil gift wrap with huge red bows. When Sammy saw them, his eyes lit up. He loved getting presents, of course, but couldn't begin to guess what the coach would have gotten all of them.

Coach Rachel whistled loudly and said, "Do not open your present until everyone has theirs. Then we'll open them at the same time."

Soon all of the presents were properly distributed, and Coach Rachel gave the signal to open them. There was a fury of tissue paper and bows flying in the air and across the table. Slowly each player began to hold his or her present up in the air to take a good look at it. Jaws began to drop around the table, and Coach Rachel was sure that meant the players were happy with their gifts.

"Well, I hope you all love your new team jerseys! I thought that if we were going to play as a team, we should really look like a team," Coach Rachel announced.

One by one, the players went over to Coach Rachel to hug and thank her for such a wonderful gift. After thanking the coach, Sammy proudly showed his family the new jersey he would wear in his first game. He would be lucky number seven. He couldn't stop smiling!

"Is this the greatest jersey you've ever seen or what?" Sammy screamed.

Dad shared in his son's joy, "Sam, that jersey is amazing. You are going to look like a real pro in it."

Sammy grinned, "I know. I love the shark on the front. It looks so…"

"Evil?" asked Stacy.

Mom laughed, "It certainly might scare the opposing team, but I don't know if it's evil."

"I think it just looks tough. Like we are going to pulverize the competition!" Sammy replied.

Andrew and Nick joined Sammy then in order to continue the conversation about their jerseys. They compared numbers and discussed how all of the other teams would be so incredibly jealous of them. Nothing would stop them from winning a trophy. Okay, maybe they'd have to play well, too. A few other team members moved toward the boys as they talked.

"How about these jerseys! Aren't they great?" asked Madeline, which made Sammy blush because any time he talked to her, he blushed.

Seeing Sammy in his frozen state, Nick replied, "You bet."

Fellow players Alexandra, Alaina and James chimed in, "Go Sharks! Go Sharks!"

The tallest of the group, Alexandra leaned on one of her crutches and looked over the crowd to see where Coach Rachel was standing. Like the rest of the team, Alexandra was already determined not to let a disability, in her case, Cerebral Palsy, stop her from being a winner at sled hockey. Noticing that the coach was not within earshot, she announced, "We should get a nice present for Coach Rachel for Christmas, too."

"That's a great idea," her best friend, Alaina, replied.

Sammy agreed, "Okay. What do you think she'd like?"

Madeline replied, "I think she really likes lighthouses. Maybe we could buy her a picture with something like that on it."

"That's a good idea, but maybe we should get her something that is more 'coach-like' or something really cool like skydiving lessons," said James, who, even though he transported himself in a wheelchair, was clearly the daredevil of the group.

Nick laughed, "Let's not put her in a body cast before she coaches our first game! I like the idea of giving her a 'coach' type of present, though."

Sammy's mother who loved to shop offered, "Why don't I try to find something for you? I'm thinking maybe a nice personalized clipboard or jacket. Something with your new Springdale Sharks logo on it."

Stacy smiled and said, "Mom, you're my shopping hero."

Coach Rachel was heading towards them so they agreed that Sammy's mother would find the present and talk to them later about it. Alexandra and Alaina bid everyone a good night before putting on their matching pink jackets and exiting the restaurant. After James left with his father, Madeline was left with Sammy, his friends and family.

"So, it's pretty great we won't have any homework for a while over Christmas break, right?" said Madeline.

"Yeah. I love Christmas break," replied Sammy.

Andrew and Nick were snickering as they watched Sammy in his conversation with Madeline, but they were careful not to let her see their enjoyment of the situation. They could see Sammy's ears turning redder and redder until they thought his head might explode. Mercifully, Madeline's parents let her know it was time to leave before Sammy fainted.

"See you guys at practice," said Madeline.

"See ya," they said.

"Okay. Knock it off, you guys." Sammy said once Madeline had left.

Nick laughed, "C'mon, Sam. She didn't see us. We think it's cute when your ears turn red."

Sammy elbowed Nick and punched Andrew in the arm, "See ya on Monday, dweebs."

As promised, Sammy's mother found a very nice present for Coach Rachel, which they presented to her at the last practice before Christmas. They could tell she was really touched by this gesture. She hugged every player and wished each a nice holiday as she wore her new embroidered coach's jacket out of the rink.

The break from schoolwork was a welcome one, and Sammy had a wonderful holiday. He received two of the hot, new video games he had asked for, and he also immensely enjoyed the new comic books that Dad had picked out for him. Selma jumped on his back as he poured over his new prize possessions. Unfortunately, her favorite toy was still one of her family members even though she had faired very well in the Christmas gift department.

Chapter 12

The next few months were busy, busy, busy. Stacy and Sammy were getting to that point in the school year where they thought—when will it be over? Sure, there were social activities, but they were also in the middle of a few big projects, and the weather was not yet warm enough and sometimes rainy.

That's why it was so fun to travel with the sled hockey team. The boys loved the fact that they now had official team jerseys with a nasty looking shark on the front. They felt the jerseys helped them to intimidate other teams. Stacy still didn't get the connection of having a shark be your mascot for a hockey team. Everyone knows that sharks swim. They don't skate or play on sleds. What good would a shark be if you took it out of the water?

They visited Philadelphia first just like Coach Rachel had mentioned. The whole family drove there together, which was rare since all of their schedules were so crazy. Stacy and Sammy had their usual arguments over what music to play, what video to watch and when to stop for a bathroom break. Surprisingly, Selma slept most of the time and was in good spirits when she was awake.

Philly was cool. They spent a lot of time at the rink where they met players from all around their tri-state area. But they also saw the Liberty Bell and ate the best cheesesteak sandwiches that they'd ever had. Every night, Sammy and his friends would hang out in the room and play video games, swim in the hotel pool or play a pick-up game of hockey in front of their hotel rooms. Sammy's family thought it was great to see him having so much fun.

Believe it or not, the Springdale Sharks actually won the tournament in Philadelphia! Coach Rachel said this was great, but that the teams in each additional tournament would be tougher so the players would need to practice more. Stacy thought Sammy and his friends might be discouraged by that announcement, but instead they were looking forward to getting a chance to play more often.

"Can you believe that we won a tournament when we've only been playing sled hockey for a few months?" Sammy gushed on their way home from Philadelphia.

Mom said, "I know. That's so great, Sammy."

"Do you like playing the position of center on the team, Sam?" Dad inquired.

"Sure."

"That's good. So, where did you guys say the next tournament will be?" asked Dad.

Stacy piped up with the answer, "Baltimore—in three more weeks."

"Looks like we'll be on the road again," chuckled Mom.

They were all looking forward to that trip, too, especially Stacy who said, "I've heard Baltimore is a really nice city with some very good shopping."

"It figures you would hear that," deadpanned Sammy.

"Leave me alone, dorko," Stacy shot back.

The family unloaded their bags and dispersed to their rooms to unpack before ordering dinner at home. Of course, everyone else was finished unpacking in record time while Stacy was still putting her makeup back in its proper place on her bedroom bureau. Sammy stopped by to watch the action on his way down to dinner.

"Maybe you'd get unpacked faster if you didn't take your entire bedroom with you for a 3-day trip," he said solemnly.

"And that would be your business, how?" Stacy retorted.

"Just an observation."

"Wow, you are using all of your vocabulary words today," Stacy squealed, "By the way, you guys were pretty great out there this weekend, but don't tell anyone that I complimented you."

He laughed, "No problem. Stacy, what do you think the other kids at school really think of sled hockey?"

"Most of them have to be impressed with what you guys are doing."

"What about everybody else?" he asked.

"Do what you think is best and don't worry about them," Stacy said, "Did one of the kids make fun of it or something?"

"Sorta."

"Who?"

"That kid, Derek. He calls me names sometimes and now that he knows about sled hockey, he's tormenting me all the time," Sammy said staring at his shoes.

"Sam, you should tell a teacher, the principal or Mom and Dad. Derek's just making fun of you to make himself look better, you know."

He continued to stare at his shoes, "I know, but it's embarrassing. Sometimes he scares me."

Stacy sat down beside of him on her bed, "Do you want to have Mom talk to Derek's parents?"

"No."

"How about if I try to stop by school one day and talk to him?"

"No."

"Sammy…how can we help?" Stacy cried.

"I don't know. I just want it to stop."

"Do Andrew and Nick know? Does he tease them, too?" Stacy asked.

Sammy thought about it, "I don't think they know. Derek always seems to make sure I'm alone when he talks to me. At the beginning of the year, I talked to Nick about Derek, but it's gotten worse since then."

"Well, maybe that's the answer. Let your friends know. Maybe he does the same thing to them. If not, at least there's safety in numbers. If all of you stick together, he won't have much of a chance," Stacy said thinking that she was pretty brilliant.

"No."

"Why not?"

"I told you. It's embarrassing," Sammy said angrily.

"Look, you are not the only person who has ever been bullied. It happened to me for a while at my old school. I found out that telling my friends so they could watch out for me was a great idea. I also told one of my teachers, too. It didn't stop for a while, but it did eventually," Stacy said.

"When?"

Stacy punched him lightly, "When the bully finds someone else to torture. It's sad, but it usually works that way."

"Why do people have to be so mean?" he asked.

"Some people are mean. Most are nice. Just tell Nick and Andrew the next time you see them," Stacy begged.

"Okay. I promise I will."

Chapter 13

Soon they traveled to Baltimore for Sammy's next tournament. This time Nick's parents couldn't come so he rode with Stacy and Sammy's family. Do you know how annoying two 11-year-old boys can be when they are in a minivan together for more than an hour? Good grief.

"Will you guys calm down? With all that noise, it's hard for anyone to think straight," Stacy complained.

"When did you start thinking? That must be a new skill for you," Sammy jabbed back.

Stacy snarled, "Knock it off or I'll…"

"No threats, Stacy. And Sammy, quiet down a little bit," Mom interrupted then promptly changed the subject, "What do you think of eating at one of the restaurants at the Inner Harbor tonight?"

Sammy groaned, "Is fish all they have to eat?"

"No, there will be plenty of food for you to choose from," Mom replied.

"Have you ever gone fishing, Sam?" Nick asked.

"No."

"Well, if you go and catch anything, you sorta have to try it. I did and it wasn't bad at all," said Nick.

"Really?"

"Sure. And I even learned a joke that's sorta about fishing," said Nick.

"What?"

"I'm on a seafood diet. I see food and I eat it," replied Nick.

Stacy groaned, "That's not even a joke."

Nick continued his story without responding, "Anyway, my uncle took me fishing last summer. You should go with us sometime. The only bad thing was that we ran into that creep Derek from school. He was there with his dad."

Stacy remembered her earlier conversation with Sammy about Derek and asked, "Nick, does he ever pick on you at school?"

"Sure. Not as much as he used to. He must've found a new target."

"Yeah—me!" cried Sam.

"Seriously? I didn't know that," Nick said in amazement, "I mean, I've never even seen the two of you together."

"I know. He waits until I'm by myself to talk to me. He calls me 'Slow Sammy' mostly. And he threatens to hit me if I tell anybody," Sammy sighed.

"Sam, you should have told your dad and I about that. I can talk to your teacher as soon as we get back from Baltimore," Mom turned to look at him with concern.

"No! That will make things worse. Please don't do that!" Sammy practically screamed.

"But..."

"No. Please..." Sammy pleaded with her.

Nick interjected, "He might be right, Mrs. R. It probably would get worse. You, Andrew and I can just stick together and make sure Derek doesn't catch up with you when you're by yourself. I have some older friends who can beat him up if they have to."

"Nick, you can't do that. Then you'll be just as bad as he is," Mom replied.

"Okay. Then we'll just make sure we watch out for Sam! There's no way he'll hurt you if there are a bunch of us looking out for you," Nick said patting Sammy on the shoulder.

"What did I tell you, Sam? I think you have an intelligent big sister who gave you the same advice recently," Stacy smiled.

Everyone laughed as Stacy continued to praise herself at how smart she was. Before they knew it, they were in Baltimore and having dinner near the water. The view was beautiful, and the boys talked nonstop about their upcoming games. No one was even thinking about Derek then.

Chapter 14

The Springdale Sharks played three hard-fought games before entering the rink to play in the championship game of the Baltimore tournament. Sam was now playing on a line with Nick, Andrew, Alaina and James. The goalie was Alexandra. The teammates were getting used to playing together so they had slowly developed a rhythm that was helping them to pass and score as a team.

The first two periods of the championship game were relatively uneventful. Each team scored one goal. As the third period began, Sammy glided onto the ice looking a bit tired. After losing the first face-off, he seemed even more discouraged. Most of the third period went on in this lackluster manner.

In the last time-out before the end of the game, Sammy's family could see Coach Rachel and Assistant Coach Joel giving their best pep talk to the players. Shortly thereafter, the opposing team shot several pucks at Alexandra, but she was able to deflect every one as the crowd cheered her on.

The excitement in the arena was building with only one minute to go in the final period. Sammy and his line took to the ice again for what might be the last time. The fans seemed to be holding their collective breath as Sammy won the face-off this time.

"I don't think I can watch this!" Stacy practically screamed.

"I know. I'm on the edge of my seat," Mom laughed.

Selma even seemed to sense the excitement. She stopped playing with her favorite doll and watched the players on the ice intently. Dad was biting his fingernails and tapping his foot. They were all so nervous for Sammy and his friends.

Just then they noticed Sammy turn his sled abruptly near the goal and pass the puck to his teammate, Alaina. She quickly responded and with a flick of her wrist, shot the puck into the goal. The buzzer sounded and everyone screamed. Alaina had scored the winning goal and Sammy had assisted.

"I can't believe it! Go Sharks! Go Sharks!" Stacy started to chant and stomp her feet.

The crowd joined Stacy in the chant, and Sammy moved toward the glass and raised his hockey stick up to them. He turned to join the rest of the team as they lined up to say 'good game' to the opposing team. It was almost hard to believe the Sharks had won, but they had, and everyone in the stands was incredibly happy for them.

Stacy turned to Mom and noticed a tear in her eye, "Mom, are you okay?"

"Yes," she whispered.

"What...?"

"You know, when Sammy was born I didn't think he would ever play any sport. He's had so many surgeries and I can't even count how many tests and doctor visits anymore, but just look at him out there now," Mom smiled.

"I know," Stacy said hugging her.

Dad and Selma joined in the family hug as Dad said, "We'd better go see how our little athlete is doing."

They all left their seats and walked to the locker rooms. Even standing outside, Sammy's family could hardly hear themselves think. The players were screaming and talking and laughing all at the same time when they came out into the hallway. Coach Rachel saw Sammy's family out of the corner of her eye and walked to where they were standing.

"Well, what do you think of your Sammy now?" Coach Rachel asked.

"Amazing," Mom replied, "All of these kids are amazing."

Coach Rachel nodded, "I think so, too. This has got to be the best job I've ever had."

"Next stop?" Dad inquired with a smile.

"Columbus, Ohio."

"Who would've known we'd travel to so many places all in one year?" Mom laughed.

Even though it was very early when they pulled away from the hotel the next morning, they chatted feverishly in the minivan. The boys discussed their strategy for Columbus. Selma watched her favorite video, but broke into the conversation occasionally with a yelp. Mom, Dad and Stacy talked about how much they had liked Baltimore.

Although their time in Baltimore had been short, they managed to visit the Inner Harbor, including the aquarium and the science center. Plus the food there was great. The city was definitely on their "must see again" list. And Columbus would be on their "must see soon" list now!

Chapter 15

The trip to Columbus was great fun, too. This time they got the opportunity to go out to dinner with the entire team and their family members. They hadn't had a chance to do that since their Christmas celebration. Everyone was happy to be getting to know each other better. They were starting to become like an extended family of sorts.

Unfortunately, at this tournament, the Sharks lost one game and tied one game. The players had never seemed so disappointed. Since they hadn't been losing, they really hadn't learned how to lose very well. It wasn't pretty at first, but Coach Rachel set things straight in her typical down-to-earth fashion.

She stared at the players for what seemed like an eternity as she began her speech before their next game, "The Springdale Sharks have not done as well in Columbus as in the other cities we've visited. What do you think that means?"

"These teams are too tough for us to beat," answered Alaina sadly with her sidekick Alexandra nodding in agreement.

"Yeah, they're better than we are," James added with an unusual look of defeat. It was not like James to admit defeat.

Sammy tried to see the bright side of this mess, "Maybe we just need more practice. We could beat these teams next year!"

"Next year?" asked Coach Rachel.

"Right. We're done for this year, aren't we? There's no way we could win now. We've lost one and tied one," said Nick matter-of-factly.

Coach Rachel smiled, "Well, thanks for keeping track of that information, guys. But I have a little surprise for you. One of the teams has had a couple of injuries and is forfeiting. That means if you win this game, you can still have a shot at playing in the playoff and championship game."

"No way!" shouted Andrew.

"Way," laughed Coach Rachel, "Please don't give up yet, guys. I think you have a real shot at winning this tournament. And that means you'll go to the championship game for our region. That is unbelievable for a first-year team, and I think you are good enough to do it!"

"Then, we have to do it!" Alexandra exclaimed.

Everyone began chanting 'Let's Go Sharks' as the team took to the ice. The players' families were all in the stands and ready to make some noise. They brought posters, pompoms and cowbells that sounded in your ears for minutes after they were rung.

The first period was bad. The second one was worse. Even Coach Rachel looked solemn as the team got back onto the ice for the third and final period. Whack...slam...crunch. This game was not pretty and for the first time since Sammy began playing sled hockey, Mom was a little worried that he might get hurt. The team they were playing had players that seemed much bigger than the Sharks.

With ten minutes to go, the Sharks were behind by one goal. Not promising. A puck was headed straight toward Alexandra's head, but she managed to reject it and deny the other team's goal. This super save seemed to cause a surge of energy in the players. Suddenly, they looked ready to go down fighting.

"Wow. Did they just get better all of a sudden?" Stacy asked Dad.

"Looks like they've got a last minute rush of energy," he replied.

"They needed it!"

Before they knew it, the Sharks had scored a goal to bring the game to a tie. The crowd was wild now. There were two minutes left in the game. Could the Sharks pull off another last minute win again?

Unfortunately, the answer was 'no.' The game ended in a tie. The announcer let everyone know that due to time limitations, there would be a 'shoot out.' This meant that each team would pick their three best players to shoot for the goal. Whichever team had scored the most goals would then win the game.

The Sharks picked Sammy, Alaina and Nick. The opposing team's first player took a shot and scored. No pressure here now! Sammy took a shot and missed. He was so disappointed. During the second round of action, the opposing team missed the goal, but Alaina scored. Tied again!

This was it. The game would be over after the third round. The opposing team's player slid into place, shot the puck hard to the left and missed the goal. Now Nick was up. He didn't look confident. In fact, Sammy thought Nick looked like he might throw up at any minute. Nick evaluated the goalie briefly and flipped the puck up in the air and to the right. The goalie missed! Nick had scored the winning goal!

Everyone rushed to Nick's side to congratulate him on his amazing play and shout, "Nick is number one! Nick is number one! Let's go Sharks!"

What a great ending to a tough tournament! It was certain that none of the players would forget their play in Columbus anytime soon. The players glided to the edge of the ice and planned for their victory celebration.

Chapter 16

Back at school, the Springdale Sharks players were beginning to get noticed. The principal spoke about the team's win during the morning announcements on Monday prompting everyone in Sammy's class to clap for the team. Well, everyone except Derek.

It seemed the more attention that the team got, the angrier that Derek appeared. It was starting to scare Sammy a little bit. Most of the time, he hung out with the other guys, and Derek left him alone. But sometimes, he was alone and that was when Derek somehow found him.

"Nice announcement this morning," Derek stared at Sammy as he stood near his locker before lunch.

"Yeah," Sammy said quietly.

Derek leaned against one of the lockers casually and said, "So you think you're pretty hot stuff, right now?"

"No."

"Aw, c'mon! Slow Sammy is finally becoming the school hero. It must feel really good," Derek's words dripped wth sarcasm.

Sammy was feeling flushed now. He was tired of being afraid of Derek. He was more than a little sick of his snide comments. He knew if he started a fight that he would not be physically capable of fin-ishing it. And he knew that he would probably get kicked off of the team just before the championship game next week. He almost didn't care.

Sammy snarled at Derek, "Look, we worked really hard to get where we are. I'm proud of that. I guess it makes you feel really big to call me Slow Sammy. I'm glad that gives you such a kick, but I really have to get to lunch now."

"Whoa...you're mighty brave all of a sudden," Derek frowned, "If I were you, I would be very careful."

Sammy felt the anger welling up in his chest. He felt like he might cry, but managed to shout, "Sure. I guess you'll beat me up. That should be easy for you since I'm Slow Sammy. No challenge there! Why don't you go beat up an old lady, too!"

Derek seemed a bit stunned by this response, "I'm warning you..."

"Derek, if you plan to hit me, do it now. I want to get on with my life. Even if you knock me out completely, I'll probably get up and still finish the school year and go to my tournament. Do you think you'll have a shot at staying in school if you hit me? Or maybe that's why you want to hit me...because you are such a loser that you can't handle being in school."

Derek was clenching his fists now so Sammy expected to get punched at any second. It was obvious that no one had ever both-ered to say something like this to Derek before. Or maybe no one had ever been that stupid. It was amazing that not one person had entered the hallway where they stood since their conversation began.

"Did you just call me a loser?" Derek squeaked.

Sammy knew there was no backing down now, but he did regret calling him a loser. Who knew why Derek acted the way he did? It wasn't very nice to call anyone that. Mom would probably say that Derek might have terrible problems at home and that could be why he acted the way he did.

"Derek, I've never wanted to call you names or be your enemy, but you have tortured me since my first day of school."

"Don't try to take it back now. It's too late," Derek snarled.

"Okay then. Just hit me and get it over with. I'm starving, and I want to go to lunch," Sammy said coldly.

"No. I think I'll wait. A surprise attack is always more fun. If I were you, I'd keep my eyes open," said Derek.

"Whatever," Sammy said and walked away.

Sammy's heart was pumping so fast that he thought he would stop breathing. He couldn't believe some of the things he had said to Derek. He was sure that their hate-hate relationship had not ended, but he was glad that he said the things he said. Even if there was a surprise attack in his future, Sammy was happy that he had finally defended himself.

Chapter 17

Sammy told Nick and Andrew about his little encounter with Derek at lunch. The boys renewed their vow to watch out for one another. Sammy was happy he had found such good friends at school this year, and that feeling took away some of the fear he had that Derek might pulverize him at any minute.

Andrew changed the subject with one look at his sandwich, "Well, it's mystery meat again. I'm pretty sure the lunch ladies are stealing small animals from the neighborhood and using them to feed us."

Nick laughed and said, "I think you're right. I haven't seen the poodle that lives next door to us in over a week."

Sammy took a bite and added, "Well, if it is your neighbor's poodle, she tastes just like chicken."

The boys snorted with laughter until the kids around them began to stare. Their Springdale Shark teammates Alaina and Alexandra heard the commotion and headed to their table. As usual, they had similar outfits on, and each had their hair in a ponytail. They didn't look so cheerful.

"What's wrong?" asked Nick.

"In gym class this morning, James was reaching for the ball during a game of dodgeball. He fell over in his wheelchair and broke his arm!"

"No way!" exclaimed Sammy.

"It's true. And that means he won't be able to play in our championship game. We have to add someone else to our line," Alexandra said.

"This stinks. How will we win when we haven't played together?" Sammy asked.

"Do you know who we're adding?" asked Andrew.

"Yep," Alaina smiled.

"C'mon! Tell us!" Nick pleaded.

"Madeline," said Alexandra.

Sammy blushed. He always blushed when he thought about Madeline. Sure, they were on the same team, but if she played on his line, they would be inseparable. It might be very distracting.

"She's not a bad player," Nick responded carefully.

"Are you sure you don't have any comments about her being a girl?" asked Alaina clenching her fists as if she were going to pounce on him if he answered incorrectly.

"No!" the boys said in unison.

"Okay then. Let's see if Coach Rachel will get us some extra ice time so we can work with Madeline as much as possible," Alexandra replied in her usual take charge manner.

The lunch bell rang saving Sammy from further conversation about Madeline. He was surprised at how much had happened to him within an hour. He was thinking back to his hallway talk with Derek with a little fear in his heart. But he was also thinking of spending extra time with Madeline.

The afternoon dragged on after such excitement in the late morning. Sammy didn't see Derek again until the end of the day. Since Mom was picking Sammy up from school to drive to the rink, he had hoped they could make a quick getaway. Fortunately, Sammy did make it to the minivan to greet Mom before Derek walked over to him. Mom saw how Sammy watched Derek's every move even after they were in the minivan together.

"Who is that boy, Sam?" Mom asked.

"What boy?" Sammy tried to be nonchalant.

"The one you were staring at."

"Derek."

Mom looked at him with a wrinkled brow, "Is something going on between the two of you?"

"No."

"Is he the bully you were talking about?"

"What?" Sammy exclaimed.

"You heard what I said. Is he being mean to you?" Mom asked.

"He's mean to everyone," Sammy said.

"But you've been having a problem with him," Mom continued.

Sammy couldn't take this line of questioning any more. He gave in and told Mom everything that had happened before lunch. He was surprised that he told her everything, but once the words poured out of his mouth, he couldn't stop them. And it did feel better to have told her about what happened.

Mom was calmer than Sammy thought she would be as she asked, "How can I help with this now?"

"I don't know," Sammy started to cry.

"Honey..." Mom sobbed and put her hand on his shoulder. "What about..."

"Mom, I stood up for myself today. If that doesn't stop Derek, nothing will. Okay?" Sammy sighed.

"Okay."

"One of our players broke his arm today so we'll be getting someone new on our line," Sammy changed the subject quickly.

"Really? Who?" Mom asked.

"Madeline."

"Oh, I've met her and her parents. She seems really nice," Mom added.

"Well, she seems like a good player. We're going to ask if we can get some extra practice time to start working with her on some plays."

Mom smiled, "You guys are becoming quite a well-oiled machine. I'm very impressed with your dedication."

Mom and Sammy chatted about sled hockey until they got to the rink where Coach Rachel made the official announcement about James' unfortunate injury. Madeline seemed nervous about the move, but she did well during practice. As promised, Alaina and Alexandra asked about getting extra ice time to practice and Coach Rachel agreed. They were set to practice again on Saturday morning.

Stacy could tell by the way that Sammy looked at Madeline that he liked her in the same way that she liked her favorite hockey player, Ben. So, once Stacy learned Sam and Madeline would be playing together, she teased Sam mercilessly when no one else was around later that evening. He also told her about the Derek incident, and she began to worry again about how safe Sammy really was at his school.

Chapter 18

The next two weeks were filled with practice, practice and more practice. The school held a pep rally to celebrate the team's success and wish them well before the Springdale Sharks were off to Buffalo, New York for the championship game of the season.

They had a great time seeing Niagara Falls from both the American and Canadian sides of the water. While Sammy and his teammates fit in some much needed practice, Mom and Stacy did what they do best—shop! That was all on Friday. Then on Saturday, the players and their families ate brunch together a few hours before the big game.

Anticipation was in the air as they dined that morning. The parents were chatting while most of the players joked around and almost started a food fight. Toward the end of the meal, Coach Rachel stood up to say a few words.

"Well, here we are just before the championship game. I am amazed at what you players have been able to accomplish this year, and I can't begin to tell you how proud I am of you. I just want you to know that I think you really have a great shot at winning today, but you will still be amazing to me whether or not we take home a trophy."

Stacy smiled and glanced over at Sammy who was beaming with pride. Coach Rachel was right. These kids were pretty amazing—when they weren't annoying. Just as she was feeling all warm and fuzzy about her little brother, he threw a small container of butter at her. It hit her square in the nose and bounced right into her glass of water.

"Sammy!" Mom reprimanded him before Stacy had a chance to reach over the table and beat the snot out of him, "Knock it off or you'll be sitting in the hotel room this afternoon instead of at the rink."

Sammy sheepishly got up from the table and followed the other players out of the restaurant. He didn't want to ruin his shot at playing in the game, but he was pretty psyched at what wonderful aim he had today. He climbed in the minivan and they all headed to the rink. Sammy's family took their seats behind the glass at the edge of the rink.

"This rink is freezing," complained Stacy.

"Well, Sammy is playing ice hockey. What else would you expect?" Dad inquired.

Stacy rolled her eyes, "I mean this rink is colder than some of the other rinks we've been to lately. There must not be any heat at all!"

"I agree," Mom responded sympathetically.

"You know, I feel like I've been to so many sled hockey games lately that I could give a play-by-play of the game," Stacy continued complaining.

Dad laughed, "Are you sure about that? From what I've seen, you usually come to the rink for 10 minutes, leave to get hot chocolate, come back and talk to whoever you can find to sit with then continue that cycle until the end of the game."

"Oh, you forgot that usually in the second period of the game, she adds the purchase of a pretzel," Mom said.

"Okay. Maybe I'll just stick to being in the crowd," Stacy giggled.

Stacy continued with her typical pattern of talking and eating until the third period. Then she decided to watch Sammy play because she felt guilty for not having watched him play at the beginning of the game. It was a good thing that she started paying attention because this time the final period of the game was awesome!

The Sharks and their opponents were moving so fast that you could forget they were on sleds. It was just like watching a regulation hockey game. Anyone who worried about Madeline doing well as she played with Sam, Andrew, Nick, Alaina and Alexandra shouldn't have been concerned. She kicked butt!

With two minutes left in the game, the Sharks were winning. By this time, Sammy's family was jumping up and down in the stands and screaming along with the rest of the crowd. Nick had the puck and passed it with ease to Sammy who was within a few feet of the net. He flipped the puck in the air and shot it toward the goal. The red light flashed and they knew that he had scored a goal.

Sammy backed his sled up a bit and threw his arms into the air in celebration. He could not believe he had just scored what may very well be the game-winning goal since there wasn't much time left on the clock. Just then Sammy saw a strange look on Nick's face. It was as if Nick was trying to say something to him from across the ice, but the words couldn't come out fast enough. As if in slow motion, Sammy turned his head and saw the referee falling toward him. Sammy must've bumped into him when he backed up his sled causing him to lose his balance.

It was too late to move or even protect himself. Within seconds, the ref had landed on Sammy and his sled. Sammy felt an incredible weight and sharp pain on his back. He was having trouble breathing and it seemed like an eternity before anyone helped him.

"Sam, are you okay?" Madeline cried.

"Sam…" Nick didn't know what to say.

The players were cleared from the ice, and Sammy's parents were now near him while Stacy sat in the stands with Selma singing to her. You could hear a pin drop in the rink. Everyone was focused on Sammy who was still lying on the ice as one of the paramedics checked him out. Tears rolled down the faces of his teammates, but they didn't notice them.

The paramedics lifted Sammy onto a stretcher. By then he seemed okay because he waved at the crowd. Mom came back to her seat. She looked worried, but calmer than when she had left Stacy and Selma.

"What's going on?" Stacy asked.

"They think he is just bruised up a bit, but we're going to the hospital for x-rays. Believe it or not, he wants to see the rest of the game and then go since there are only a couple of minutes left," Mom laughed nervously.

"And you are letting him do that?" Stacy asked with shock.

"Yes. This means a lot to him, and we'll leave within 5 minutes."

The game ended with a championship win for the underdog team of the year—the Springdale Sharks. What a season! Sammy's family didn't stay long enough for the trophy presentation, but his friends visited him at the hospital later. According to Sammy, seeing them was the best prize of all.

Alaina asked, "How ya feeling, Sam?"

"Sore, but I'm happy we won," he giggled.

"Now you'll go down in history for being our first player ever hurt in a tournament game!" said Nick.

Mom winced, "I'm not sure that's how you want to be remembered, but let me just say that all of you were great today. I'm so glad you stopped by to see Sammy."

"Do you have to stay overnight?" Madeline asked.

Sammy blushed at her concern, "No. It sounded like I just need to get checked out and then we can go."

They were all relieved that Sam's injury had turned out to be nothing major. Sammy was gleaming because they would be returning to Springdale as champions.

Chapter 19

Back at school, Sam and his teammates became heroes—at least for the remainder of the school year. Even Derek congratulated Sam on his team's win at one point. In the back of his mind, Sammy thought Derek would change back to his old self soon, but he didn't worry much about it then.

Just a few days before the wrapup of their school year, the principal of their school decided to hold a Community Appreciation Day for the Springdale Sharks. Everyone in town was invited to the school grounds for a huge picnic, including outdoor games and music. There were hundreds of balloons in their team colors decorating one of the biggest parties that Sammy had ever attended.

"Can you believe the principal planned all of this?" Andrew said in amazement.

Sammy's mom replied, "Well, your team has brought a lot of positive attention to our community. You all deserve a special day like this."

"Yeah. This is great. Did you see Selma? She's having a blast, too," Sammy said as they observed his sister engrossed in a fierce game of 'tag—you're it.'

Stacy agreed, "Selma always has a good time wherever she goes, but I think she is really loving some of the kids' games they have here."

As if she had heard what they were saying, Selma hopped over to Sammy and Stacy, "Go slide."

"Sure, Selma. In just a little while," replied Stacy.

"Slide now," Selma answered as she pulled on Stacy's hand.

Stacy leaned down to whisper in Selma's ear, "Not right now. I have to make a big speech in just a minute."

Selma frowned and headed toward Dad. She was sure he would play with her. Stacy walked toward the big stage that had been set up in the middle of the courtyard of Sammy's school. She walked up a few steps, ran her hand through her hair to smooth it and approached the microphone at center stage.

"What's going on?" asked Sammy.

"It looks like Stacy is going to make a little speech," Mom replied nonchalantly.

Sammy giggled, "You're kidding, right? Why would she make a speech today?"

Mom elbowed Sam and smiled, "We'll have to wait and see, Mr. Patience."

By this time, Andrew, Nick, Alexandra, Alaina, Madeline and James had gathered near Sammy since they knew what Stacy was about to say. They were excited at knowing about this surprise and having kept if from Sammy for more than two weeks. Alexandra and Alaina in particular had exhibited incredible restraint since there was nothing they liked better than sharing a secret.

Stacy began her speech...

As everyone knows, this year we were all honored to be part of an unbelievable journey as the Springdale Sharks went from being a bunch of kids just learning how to move along the ice to a team of champions.

Not only has the team been an inspiration to me, but there is one player in particular that I truly admire—my brother, Sam.

So what exactly is so admirable about him? First, he is one of the strongest people that I've ever met. I'm not talking about physical strength. I'm talking about strength of character. He is a person who knows who he is, including any of his limitations, and always remains true to his heart. He doesn't buckle under peer pressure. He never treats someone in any way that he would not want to be treated.

He also has a great sense of humor. He can laugh at himself, and also has the ability to laugh with you about your own mistakes—not at you. Well, sometimes, he does laugh at me. After all, he is my little brother and that's what they're supposed to do!

The audience laughed and nodded in agreement as Stacy continued...

But the trait that I most admire about him is the fact that he tries. He never gives up. And when he fails, he picks himself up and tries again.

Sam was born with a birth defect, but being physically challenged hasn't slowed him down one bit. He is a daily inspiration in my life. He teaches me what's important and what's worth fighting for. I would love and respect him even if he wasn't my brother. But I'm really glad that he is.

Sammy didn't know that I would be speaking today. I'm sure he's a bit surprised because he doesn't usually hear me say many nice things about him—especially when we are fighting over the bathroom in the morning!

And, Sammy, we have one more surprise for you now, too. Coach Rachel has an announcement to make.

Coach Rachel joined Stacy on the stage and began her big announcement...

As some of you may know, Sammy was injured in our championship game and was unable to attend the awards ceremony after the game. Today, we are here to give out the award he should have received weeks ago. The award for Most Valuable Player goes to Samuel Richardson! Sammy, please come get your trophy.

Sammy could not believe his ears! Most Valuable Player! This was unbelievable. He walked toward the stage in a fog, feeling like it was really someone else who had won and he just dreamed up the entire thing. But, he had really won. Coach Rachel hugged him and gave him a huge trophy that had his name engraved on it. The crowd clapped so hard that the noise was deafening.

As they all began to walk off of the stage, Stacy put her arm around Sammy's shoulders, "Congratulations, Sam."

"Thanks! And thanks for saying all that nice stuff about me."

"No problem. Today is your day—but tomorrow we go back to our usual routine!" Stacy laughed, "Should I meet you at 8:30 tomorrow morning for our usual fight over the bathroom?"

"I'll be there!" Sammy laughed.

By now, his teammates were signaling to him that he should go with them to the basketball court for a quick game and to show off his trophy. Sammy signaled to Mom and Dad that he was heading there then he gave Stacy a quick hug, not wanting anyone to notice that he was associating with her, but wanting to make sure she knew how much her speech had meant to him. Sammy knew there would always be more surgeries, more doctor visits and tests and more problems understanding some of his schoolwork, but now he also knew that there would always be more sled hockey and, best of all, great friends and family to help him through anything.

978-0-595-36122-9
0-595-36122-6

Printed in the United States
46187LVS00009BA/194